Mama Loved to Worry

To my mother, Barb Nieberle, champion worrier—an expert in her field. —MW

To N.C., who encourages me to always play and to tell stories with pictures. —RB

Mama Loved to Worry

Maryann Weidt  Illustrations by Rachael Balsaitis

MINNESOTA
HISTORICAL
SOCIETY PRESS

Mama loved to worry. And she had blue ribbons to prove it.

For the past two years, Mama had won the grand champion prize
for worrying at the Pickapeck County Fair.

Goodness knows she had plenty to worry about, what with Baby Eli climbing and crawling into every nook and knothole on Daisy Dell Farm.

One day Mama worried that a twister would swoop down and carry off the entire farm.

Now, sometimes, when Mama worried, she knitted. That day she knitted 347 scarves, enough for all the pigs; 295 pairs of mittens, enough for all the chickens; and 21 stocking caps, one for each of the cows.

Suddenly Mama stopped. She looked up. Clouds black as dirt tumbled tail over teakettle across the western sky. Mama scooped up Eli and ran inside.

She jumped into bed
and pulled the covers over
her head.

Finally she peeked out
and looked around.

"Now where's that Eli
gone to?" she said.

When she looked out the window,
what she saw nearly blew her
drawers clean off.

Baby Eli was climbing up the side of the silo and onto the very top of the barn. He sat up there smiling, proud as a pig in a mud puddle.

But that didn't matter one bit to the twisty wind.
It picked that toddler up, spun him around seven times,
then plunked him down in Clemson's cow pasture.

By the time Mama got to him, Eli was picking straw
out of his tiny baby teeth. Mama hoisted him up and
toted him back to the porch.

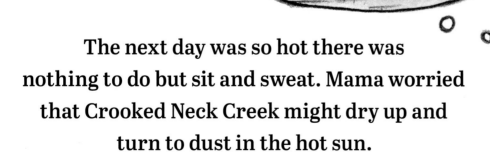

The next day was so hot there was
nothing to do but sit and sweat. Mama worried
that Crooked Neck Creek might dry up and
turn to dust in the hot sun.

Sometimes, when Mama worried, she sewed.

Mama sewed faster than a hound dog after a squirrel. She pieced together 187 paisley neckties, enough for all the uncles. She stitched 159 plaid jumpers, enough for all the aunts. She whipped up 224 polka-dot vests, enough for every one of the cousins.

And, wouldn't you know, the creek did dry up. Luckily, Mama sweated so much that a river came pouring off her. It ran smack through the middle of the farm and down to Crooked Neck Creek.

All that water caught Baby Eli's attention, and he toddled in.
He floated along and giggled and cooed.

Suddenly Mama looked around.

"Now where's that Eli gone to?" she said.

Then she spied him.

"I'm comin' to get you," she cried and dove
smack into that gully washer. She flapped her arms
like a rooster in a henhouse.

She caught hold of Eli when the young 'un got hung up
on a branch past Sullivan's swamp.

The next day turned hotter than a peck of pickled peppers. Mama worried that the heat would start the corn a poppin'.

And sometimes, when Mama worried, she cooked. She tossed together 16 tubs of sauerkraut schnitzel. She stirred up 54 pans of apricot strudel. She baked 144 dozen snickerdoodle twists.

Sure enough, it got so hot the corn popped right there in the field. It got so hot the sugar cane melted and ran down onto the popped corn.

Eli smelled something warm and sweet and headed on into that cornfield.

Mama stopped cooking and
looked around.

"Now where's that Eli
gone to?" she said.

"Guess I'm gonna have to hunt
for that boy."

First she climbed 57 feet, 3 inches, up the
side of the silo and onto the top of the
barn. She looked around.

No Eli.

Next she swam the entire length
of Crooked Neck Creek,
all 27 miles of it.

No Eli.

Finally, Mama marched up
and down the rows of corn,
all 254 acres.

There, in the middle of the very last row,
sat Eli, looking for all the
world like a roly-poly popcorn ball.

His right hand was stuck to his left ear.
His left foot was glued to the back
of his head.

"I was worried," Mama said.

She bent down to hug her baby and, you guessed it, Mama and Eli got plumb stuck together. Mama felt a worry comin' on. She looked at Eli. She looked at the two of them stuck together.

Then Mama laughed. Eli snorted. They laughed so hard they started to roll. They rolled through Clemson's cow pasture, across Sullivan's swamp, past the barn, through the yard, and smack into Crooked Neck Creek.

They splashed in the water till the pigs and chickens and cows, the uncles, aunts, and cousins all came looking for them.

"We smelled sauerkraut schnitzel," they said.

"Where have you been? We were worried."

"And hungry."

"Why worry?" Mama asked.
"Jump in."

So the pigs, chickens, and cows, the uncles,
aunts, and cousins all jumped into the creek.
They swam till the sun went down.

Then they trudged back to the farm to dry off. The pigs tossed the scarves around their necks. The chickens pulled on the mittens. The cows plunked the stocking caps on each other's heads.

The uncles put on the paisley neckties. The aunts slipped into the plaid jumpers. The cousins tried on the polka-dot vests.

They sat down to eat. They slurped and slobbered the sauerkraut schnitzel. They gobbled up the apricot strudel. They polished off the snickerdoodle twists.

Mama didn't worry there might not be enough food. She didn't worry whether everyone was having a good time. But she did worry—just a little—about who would wash all the dishes.

www.mnhspress.org
The Minnesota Historical Society Press is a member of the Association of American University Presses.
Book design by Brian Donahue / bedesign, inc.
Manufactured in Malaysia

Thanks to Greysolon Toastmasters of Duluth, who heard the story first; David LaRochelle and the Shabo children's authors, who gave it shape; and Shannon Pennefeather and the Minnesota Historical Society Press, who made it a reality. —MW

Special thanks to G.S. for chauffeuring me through southern Minnesota, and to the Gale Family Library for use of their wonderful collection of historical documents and memoirs. —RB

∞ The paper used in this publication meets the minimum requirements of the American National Standard for Information Sciences—Permanence for Printed Library Materials, ANSI Z39.48-1984.

International Standard Book Number (ISBN): 978-0-87351-994-6 (cloth)

Library of Congress Cataloging-in-Publication Data available upon request.